Dedicated to all K9s,
Law Enforcement Officers,
their children, and their
families.

Be safe always.

Did you ever stop and wonder, "What does a Police K9 and their handler do?"

Well look no further, turn the page...this is the book for you!

Their K9s are very fast, very brave, and have an amazing sense of smell!

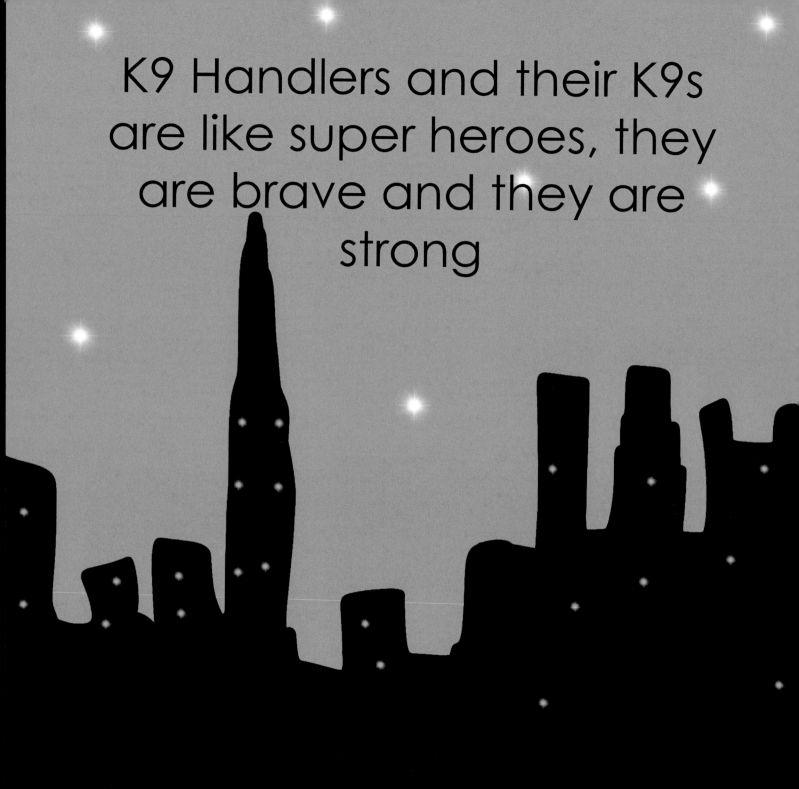

K9 Handlers and their K9s are like super heroes, they are brave and they are strong

If criminals try to run from the Police, and end up in a chase

They'll soon learn that a K9
will always win the race!

K9 Police can also help to search a scene, a home, or someone's car...

They know how to quickly find where the bad things are!

Sometimes K9s get to go
and visit kids at school

The K9 shows off his skills, and the handler explains how their job is very cool!

If you see a K9 at an airport, they are there to make sure the bags are okay

If they smell something is not right, they'll alert their handler right away!

At the end of the shift, after a very long day

A K9 looks forward to coming home with their handler to play!

They'll go to sleep and rest
their heads, but it may
not be long at all...

Because they may be needed,

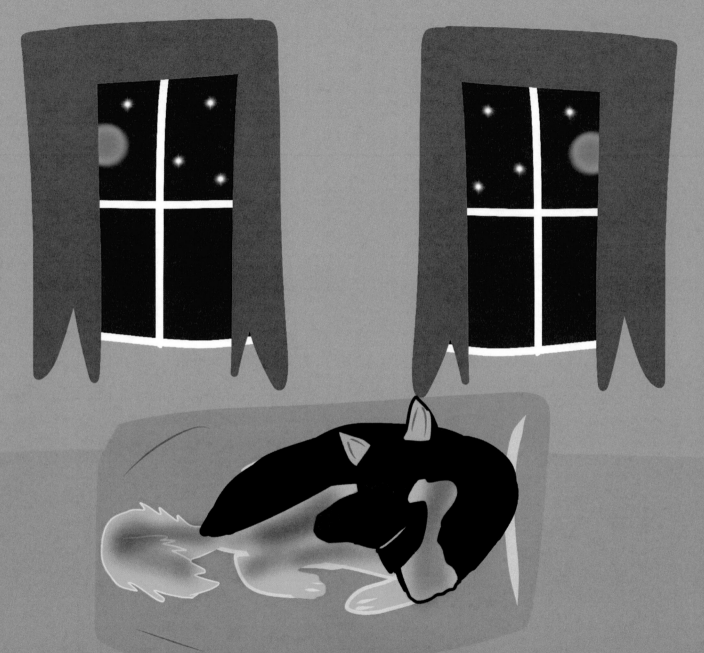

They are always on call!

So if you see a Police K9, since you now know what they do...

You can thank them for their service, and don't forget to thank their Handler too!